Princess Ponies ♡

Best Friends For Ever!

For Lucy, Jessica, Andrew and Harry

With special thanks to Julie Sykes

Bloomsbury Publishing, London, New Delhi, New York and Sydney

First published in Great Britain in January 2014 by Bloomsbury Publishing Plc
50 Bedford Square, London WC1B 3DP

Text copyright © Awesome Media and Entertainment Ltd 2014
Illustrations copyright © Jennifer Miles 2014

The moral rights of the author and illustrator have been asserted

A CIP catalogue record for this book is available from the British Library

ISBN 978 1 4088 2732 1

Typeset by Hewer Text UK Ltd, Edinburgh
Printed and bound in Great Britain by CPI Group (UK) Ltd, Croydon CR0 4YY

1 3 5 7 9 10 8 6 4 2

www.bloomsbury.com
www.ChloeRyder.com

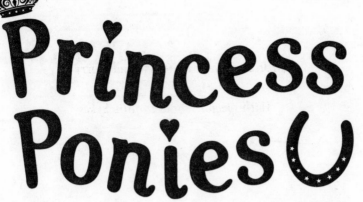

Princess Ponies

Best Friends For Ever!

CHLOE RYDER

BLOOMSBURY

LONDON NEW DELHI NEW YORK SYDNEY

The Pony

Queen
Moonshine

Princess
Crystal

Princess
Cloud

Princess
Stardust

Princess
Honey

Royal Family

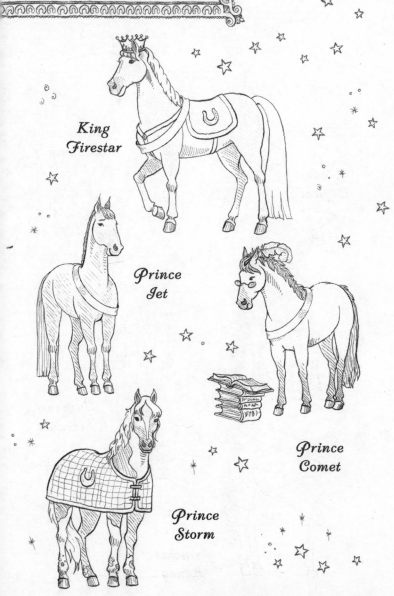

King
Firestar

Prince
Jet

Prince
Comet

Prince
Storm

Early one morning, just before dawn, two ponies stood in an ancient court-yard, looking sadly at a bare stone wall.

'In all my life this wall has never been empty. I can't believe that the horse-shoes have been taken – and just before Midsummer Day too,' said the stallion.

He was a handsome animal – a copper-coloured pony, with strong legs and bright eyes, dressed in a royal red sash.

The mare was a dainty yet majestic palomino with a golden coat and a pure white tail that fell to the ground like a waterfall.

She whinnied softly. 'We have so little time to find them all.'

With growing sadness the two ponies watched the night fade away and the sun rise. When the first ray of sunlight spread into the courtyard it lit up the wall, showing the imprints where the golden horseshoes should have been hanging.

'Midsummer Day is the longest day of the year,' said the stallion quietly. 'It's the time when our ancient horseshoes must renew their magical energy. If the horseshoes are still missing in eight days, then by nightfall on the eighth day, their magic will fade and our beautiful island will be no more.'

Sighing heavily, he touched his nose to his Queen's.

'Only a miracle can save us now,' he said.

The Queen dipped her head regally, the diamonds on her crown sparkling in the early morning light.

'Have faith,' she said gently. 'I sense that a miracle is coming.'

Chapter 1

A high-pitched cry woke Pippa. Throwing the duvet back, she was out of bed even before she'd properly opened her eyes. In the enormous bed opposite hers, Princess Stardust was tossing about, thrashing her hooves and sobbing like a little foal.

Pippa went to comfort her best friend.

'Stardust, what's wrong?'

'No,' Stardust wailed, her breath coming in noisy snorts.

Gently Pippa shook her friend awake.

'It's all right,' she soothed. 'You're safe now. It was just a bad dream.'

Stardust struggled up, sleepily squinting at Pippa through the darkness as if she couldn't quite remember who she was. Pippa smoothed a tangle of white forelock away from the Princess Pony's eyes.

'Better now?' she asked.

Stardust nuzzled at Pippa's hand.

'I was dreaming,' she said flatly. 'It was awful. It was Midsummer Day and we hadn't found all the missing horse-shoes. The moment the sun set everything went completely black and there was a terrible roaring sound. Stableside Castle collapsed and the island shrivelled up, leaving nothing but a lump of volcanic rock. All the ponies were huddled together on a tiny piece of land surrounded by sea. The tide was coming in, swirling around our hooves and rising quickly up our legs. There was nowhere to go to escape the water. Baroness Divine had wings and she flew over us, shrieking with laughter and telling us that from now on we must wear hoods and not tiaras.'

Stardust clambered out of bed, picked up a comb and half-heartedly tugged it through her mane.

'We're not going to let that happen!' Pippa said, taking the comb and brushing Stardust's mane with long, calming strokes.

'You're such a good friend,' Stardust neighed. 'And perhaps we *can* find the last horseshoe.'

Pippa hugged Stardust and walked over to the turret window.

'It's dawn,' she said, pointing at the streaks of pink that stained the dark sky.

Stardust picked up her pink jewelled tiara from the dressing table and hurriedly placed it on her head between her ears. Grabbing a cloth, she gave her hooves a quick polish. Usually Stardust spent ages getting ready so Pippa could tell that the nightmare had really frightened her.

Pippa reached for the clothes that

had magically appeared overnight and were laid out in a neat pile on the dressing table – her new outfit was a pretty stripy top and cut-off trousers.

'I'm ready,' Pippa said, shoving her feet into sandals.

Stardust hesitated at the bedroom door.

'Pippa,' she whispered, her brown eyes suddenly looking too large for her face. 'What if we don't find it in time?'

'We will,' Pippa said, her confident tone masking her own fear, 'if we work together!'

Six days ago Pippa had just arrived at the seaside for a holiday with her family when two giant seahorses magically whisked her away to Chevalia, an island inhabited by talking ponies. There she had learnt that the enchanted island was in grave danger. Eight golden horseshoes were supposed to hang on an ancient wall in the Castle courtyard. Every Midsummer Day the horseshoes' magical energy was renewed by the sun, ensuring that the island continued to thrive. But the horseshoes had been stolen and Pippa learnt that it was her quest to find them and bring them home in time for Midsummer Day. If she failed, Chevalia would fade away.

With Stardust's help she had managed to find seven of the missing horseshoes, but now Midsummer Day was here and if Pippa didn't find the last one before sunset then it would all have been for nothing. Fear gripped her stomach like an icy hand. Leading the way out of the bedroom, she set off down the turret's spiral ramp at a run.

'Breakfast first,' Stardust said, nosing open the dining-room door.

Pippa was desperate to get going but

Stardust was right – they needed a good breakfast before beginning their final search.

Pippa was surprised to find that they weren't the only early birds – Stardust's brothers and sisters were already at their feeding troughs. No one seemed to be eating much, though. Princess Crystal rolled an apple around three times without even taking a bite and Prince Comet's hot bran mash grew cold while he listlessly flicked through a book.

'It's the last day today,' Princess Honey said bravely, as Pippa and Stardust squeezed in beside her.

'Please don't start to worry yet,' Pippa said.

She was shocked by Honey's untidy appearance. Pretty Honey usually took such care of herself and was a regular customer at the Mane Street Salon, but this morning her mane was tangled and she wasn't wearing any hoof polish.

Pippa ate a dish of fresh fruit salad without tasting any of it.

'We should go up the Volcano today,' she declared. 'I bet that's where Divine has hidden the last horseshoe.'

Yesterday Stardust and Pippa discovered that it was Baroness Divine, a courtier, who had stolen the horseshoes. She foolishly believed that she could make a better life for herself without the Royal Ponies.

'That's if she hasn't already destroyed the horseshoe,' Stardust said glumly.

Comet snapped his book shut. 'I don't understand it. I thought every adult pony has read the ancient scrolls but clearly Divine hasn't,' he said. 'If she had read them then she'd know how, a long time ago, Chevalia was little more than a volcano surrounded by the sea. It's the eight golden horseshoes that allowed it to grow into the wonderful island it is today and they must have their magical energy renewed for all our sakes.'

'Peggy told me that story yesterday,' said Pippa. 'She also mentioned her friend Nightingale, the scientist-magician.'

Comet nodded. 'Yes, it was Nightingale who discovered the magical gold buried in the volcanic rock. She used it to fashion the horseshoes.'

'Mum used to tell me that story at bedtime but I thought it was just a story for little foals.' Stardust stared around the dining room. 'Where is Mum? Is she still in bed?'

'Mum and Dad were up long before us,' Crystal answered. 'I think they went to the courtyard.'

'Let's go and find them,' Stardust said, leaving most of her oaty breakfast untouched.

Queen Moonshine and King Firestar were indeed in the courtyard, standing close together and staring forlornly at the ancient Whispering Wall. Seven horseshoes sparkled in the early morning sun but, in spite of their brightness, Pippa's eyes were drawn to the gap where the eighth horseshoe should have been hanging. The bare space made her feel like a failure.

A shadow fell over the courtyard.
Glancing up, Pippa saw Princess Cloud
hovering above her in the air.

Queen Moonshine called out a greet-
ing to her daughter and Cloud swooped
lower, taking care to keep her hooves
away from the stone floor, because

touching down would mean losing her wings.

'I've got a plan,' the Queen said urgently. 'Cloud, if you rub noses with every pony on the island then, come sunset, when the island begins to fade, everyone could fly away to safety.'

'But that would take Cloud ages,' squeaked Stardust.

'And where would the ponies go?' asked Pippa.

'They could find homes in the human world,' the Queen said.

Pippa shook her head. 'Many of the ponies came here from the human world because they were neglected or treated badly there. We can't send

them back again. And it isn't over yet
– there's still time to find the last
missing horseshoe.'

'Pippa MacDonald, you've already
faced so many dangers in your quest
and Chevalia is already in your debt. It's
not right for us to ask even more of
you.'

'I'm not giving up now.' Pippa's
eyes burned with determination. 'I
promised to save Chevalia and I will!'

'Stardust,' said the Queen, 'make your
friend see sense. It's too dangerous.'

Stardust tossed her head. 'No, Mum.
Pippa is right. We can't give up now,
not when we're so close to saving
Chevalia.'

The Queen sighed in acceptance.

Reaching out, she nuzzled Stardust and Pippa closer and hugged them tight.

'Stardust, you're the bravest foal I know. And you, Pippa, are the most courageous girl.'

Pippa flushed red.

'You haven't met any other girls,' she said modestly.

'I don't have to,' the Queen said with a smile. 'So where will your search take you today?'

'The Volcano,' Pippa said immediately. 'That's where the hooded pony ran to with the horseshoes we found yesterday, which suggests the eighth one is hidden there as well.'

Pippa knew that if she said it was Divine, the apparently loyal courtier, who had stolen the horseshoes, the Queen wouldn't believe her. Pippa would have to prove it.

'Then you know your path,' said the Queen. 'Good luck, Pippa. Good luck, Stardust. Keep safe.'

Chapter 2

Pippa rode Stardust out of the Castle and over the drawbridge, towards the base of the Volcano. As they began climbing the rugged Foothills the Volcano towered above them, its fiery top illuminating the sky. Now and then a puff of smoke rose in the air, spilling red cinders that drifted over the Cloud Forest and on to the lower slopes.

'It's getting hotter the closer we get

to the Volcano,' Stardust said, stopping to catch her breath.

'I'll walk,' Pippa said, starting to slide from Stardust's back.

'No,' the Princess Pony said quickly. 'I like it when you ride me. It feels right.'

She shied, narrowly avoiding a cloud of sparks as they shot to the ground.

'Even the Volcano feels angry. Maybe this really is the end for Chevalia.'

'Never,' Pippa said vehemently.

They continued in silence and soon they entered the mysterious Cloud Forest, home to the secretive unicorns. The forest felt cool and fresh. Pippa loved the way the sunlight filtered through the ancient trees, dappling the path with golden puddles of light. Stardust slowed down, weaving a careful path through the forest to avoid the enormous vines that trailed from branches like fantastic snakes. They were over halfway through the forest when the hairs on Pippa's neck rose and her arms prickled with goosebumps. Convinced she was being watched, she looked around.

'What's wrong?' asked Stardust.

The forest around them was silent and still. As they stared into the cloudy gloom suddenly something jumped from a tree and stood on the path ahead. Stardust shied then burst out laughing.

'Misty!' she cried.

Pippa appreciated once more just

how similar Misty was to Stardust. The unicorn was almost identical to her friend, from the tilt of her head to the tip of her snow-white tail. The only differences were the pretty golden horn at the top of Misty's head and their size — Misty was the size of a large dog.

'Hello!' Misty's musical voice

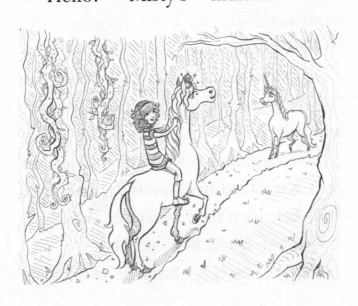

bubbled with excitement. 'Is it time already? Have you come to get us for the Midsummer Concert?'

Stardust shook her head sadly.

'I'm sorry, Misty, but there might not be a concert now. One of the horseshoes is still missing.'

'No!' Misty gasped. 'But it's Midsummer Day.'

'That's why we're here. We're on our way to the Volcano – we think the horseshoe could be hidden there,' Pippa said.

They quickly told Misty everything that had happened since the unicorns had helped them retrieve a missing horseshoe from the Cloud Forest.

'That's awful.' Misty's eyes were

wide with alarm. 'I'm coming with you.'

'It might be dangerous,' Stardust warned her.

'It'll be more dangerous if the horse-shoe isn't found,' Misty answered.

The trio set off at a brisk trot. It was fun having Misty with them. She knew the Cloud Forest like the back of her hoof and showed them a much quicker route through it. But it was still a long way.

Finally, they emerged from the treeline at the base of the Volcano and continued up its blackened slopes. The ground grew hotter and Stardust and Misty hopped from hoof to hoof, trying to avoid stepping on the lumps of hot volcanic rock. The path twisted and turned and, as they trotted round a corner, Stardust came to an abrupt halt. Misty almost ran into her and only just stopped in time. A giant river of molten lava blocked the path. Pippa turned her face away from the fiery heat rising from the bubbling red liquid.

'That was close,' Stardust said, carefully stepping backward. 'We'll have to find another way round.'

Pippa considered the bubbling lava which stretched as far as she could see in both directions.

'That could take ages,' she said. 'It would be much quicker to cross it.'

Her brain whirred with images as she tried to work out a solution. Luckily one came to her.

'Misty, could you freeze the lava with your magical horn?'

'I've never frozen something so hot before,' Misty said doubtfully. 'But I'll try.'

Bravely she stepped right up to the edge of the flowing lava.

'Careful,' Pippa warned, as a shower of sparks cascaded to the ground.

Misty lowered her head until the tip of her horn touched the lava. She winced then shied away.

'It's not working,' she said sadly. 'It's too hot and it burnt me. Plus I can sense that the lava has a magic of its own. My magic would never be strong enough to freeze it.'

As if the lava river was aware of its audience, it began to hiss. Bubbles rose to the surface, rapidly growing to the size of balloons before popping. They smelt of rotten eggs.

Stardust wrinkled her nose.

'Pooey! That's disgusting.'

'We're going to have to jump it,' Pippa said at last.

'I can't! It's too wide,' Stardust squeaked.

'But there isn't another way round.'

Stardust edged away from the hissing lava.

'I'm sorry, Pippa, but I can't. It's much too wide.'

'I bet you could if you tried. You jumped much further than this yesterday when the wild ponies taught you how to free-trot.'

Stardust stared at the molten lava rolling across their path. 'Did I?' she said in a small voice.

'Yes, you did,' Pippa said encouragingly, stroking her mane.

'But I'm scared!'

'I know,' said Pippa. 'But I've been scared so many times during our adventures and I always knew you'd help me. Why don't we practise first? My mum always says *practice makes perfect*. Look – there are lots of boulders to jump over in preparation.'

'All right,' Stardust said finally.

Turning away from the lava, she began to hop over boulders, starting with the smaller ones. Each time she cleared one Pippa cheered loudly. Misty joined in, stamping her hooves enthusiastically. Stardust's confidence grew, until soon she was jumping large boulders, clearing them with ease.

'Faster!' urged Misty. 'The faster you run at the jump the easier it is. Watch me.'

Misty galloped towards a boulder almost twice her height. She cleared it with a triumphant flick of her hind hooves. Stardust stared in amazement. Singling out a boulder almost three times her height, she pawed at the ground then took off at a gallop.

'Brilliant!' Pippa shouted, as Stardust cleared the boulder with half a metre to spare.

Stardust pulled up, her sides heaving as she struggled to catch her breath.

'I'm ready,' she said when she was breathing normally again.

A shiver of fear ran down Pippa's spine. Now that the moment had come to jump the lava river *she* didn't want to do it.

Swallowing back her panic, she said, 'Let's do it for Chevalia!'

Stardust circled away from the lava river. She went so far away from it that for a second Pippa wondered if she was running away. Then she turned on her hind hooves. Taking a deep breath, she put her head down and galloped flat out towards the lava. A stride's length away she sprang, muscles bunching as she launched herself skyward. Pippa's face and arms glowed in the fiery heat beneath her. She held her breath, hardly daring to look down. Stardust hit the ground with a thump and galloped

several strides before she was able to
pull up.

'We did it,' she gasped.

'*You* did it,' Pippa corrected her.

'We!' Stardust shouted to make her
voice heard over Misty's triumphant
cheers. 'That was teamwork. I could
never have done it without your help.'

'We help each other all the time,'
said Pippa.

'I know,' Stardust said happily. 'It's
what best friends do.'

'It's my turn now,' called Misty.

Stardust turned to watch the little
unicorn run at the lava. Her golden
horn bobbed up and down as she
pounded towards the molten river.
There was a determined glint in her eye

as she took off. She cleared the lava in one giant leap and her smile was brighter than the morning sun as she landed gracefully.

Pippa and Stardust cheered but there was no time to rest. The three friends continued steadily up the Volcano.

'How much further?' Stardust asked.

'We're nearly there,' said Misty.

As the climb became steeper, Stardust and Misty fell silent, saving their energy for the ascent. Sweat trickled from Pippa's scalp and ran down her forehead into her eyes. Her curls felt limp, like seaweed stranded on the beach. She pushed them back from her face. What would they find at the top of the Volcano? With the hungry, red flames belching skyward it was hard to imagine anything existing up there at all. The path continued to twist until, rounding another bend, Stardust drew up sharply.

'What's that?'

'It's a castle!' Pippa said, her heart thudding against her ribs.

Ahead of them was the biggest castle she'd ever seen, built into the face of the Volcano. Its turrets loomed above them, with their tall, slit windows staring out like all-seeing eyes. Ebony towers and turrets spiked upward from behind a solid jet wall. A massive drawbridge was drawn up, preventing intruders from crossing a moat of bubbling orange-red lava and reaching an enormous, coal-coloured door.

The whole place had a forbidding look. Even the craggy stone walls seemed to shout, '*Go away!*'

Stardust gave a huge, sad sigh.

'I don't believe it. We've come all this way and now we can't get in.'

Chapter 3

Pippa squinted, scanning the Volcano Castle for a way in. She spotted guard ponies peering down over the walls.

'Look,' she said, pointing. 'The guards have seen us. They're lowering the drawbridge.'

Two stern-faced Night Mares, wearing black sashes encrusted with diamonds, were letting the drawbridge down.

'Why would they do that straight away,' Pippa mused, 'unless they're expecting us?'

'You mean it could be a trap?' Stardust asked, her voice squeaky with fear.

'Maybe – perhaps Divine guessed that we'd come after her.'

'We don't have to go in,' Misty said, taking dainty steps backward.

'We do,' said Pippa. 'It's our best chance of finding the last horseshoe.'

As the drawbridge clanged down over the moat, the guard ponies motioned for them to cross it and come up. Stardust stepped forward and, after a hoof beat's hesitation, Misty followed. The flapping of wings made Pippa look up.

Something soared overhead and was

gone in a flash. She gazed at the sky but there was nothing there. She gripped on to Stardust's mane as the Princess Pony trotted across the rattling drawbridge.

'Welcome, strangers,' neighed the guards.

'Hello,' Stardust whinnied back. 'Please can we come in?'

The Night Mares exchanged a grin.

'Of course,' said the taller one. 'It's a pleasure to have you here. It's not often that we get to welcome visitors.'

Pippa could feel Stardust quivering beneath her. Taking a deep breath to steady her own trembling hand, she patted Stardust's neck. Bravely Stardust stepped up into the castle, which appeared to be the home of the Night Mares. Having passed through the enormous door they found themselves in a courtyard.

'It's just like the one back home, only there's no Whispering Wall,' exclaimed Stardust.

'There's no wall at all,' said Pippa.

The courtyard stretched away and

opened out into a long, stone balcony
that overhung a huge pool of bubbling
lava. Tearing her eyes away from the
smouldering pool, Pippa stared upward
and glimpsed the blue sky dotted with
fluffy, white clouds.

'This must be the heart of the
Volcano,' she whispered.

Her eyes widened as she took in their
surroundings. The lava pool was indeed
the very centre of the Volcano, with a
whole world carved into the rock
around it. Pippa saw caves of all sizes
linked by walkways of black stone.
There were spires decorated with scary,
stone pony gargoyles that spat rivers of
molten lava into the pit below. There
were graceful arches and stone pillars

all elaborately carved with the heads of ponies. The lava pool lit the caves, turrets and arches with a soft red glow. Pippa shivered despite the heat.

'Look how busy everyone is,' Misty said in wonder.

Ponies bustled about, nodding to each other as they hurried past. Pippa gripped Stardust's mane as two familiar ponies trotted by.

'Look!' she gasped. 'That's Nightshade and Eclipse.'

'Hey, you!' Stardust shouted. 'You stole our first horseshoe.'

Several ponies stopped and stared but Stardust ignored them and kept shouting until Nightshade turned around. She trotted over, closely followed by Eclipse.

'We did not,' she said indignantly. 'The Mistress gave us that horseshoe. She said it belonged to her and that we must hide it for a game.'

'That's not true,' Stardust said, shaking her head. 'The Mistress stole all eight horseshoes from the Royal Family. She took them from our ancient Whispering Wall, where they've hung for centuries.'

'Are you sure?' asked Eclipse. 'But the Mistress is our loyal protector – she wouldn't steal anything.'

'The horseshoes belong here, where they were made,' Nightshade argued.

'They were made here,' agreed Stardust, 'but they truly belong on the Whispering Wall. It's written in the

ancient scrolls. If you don't believe me then check.'

'Ancient scrolls? I've never heard of any scrolls,' Nightshade said. 'And you shouldn't go around shouting at ponies that they're thieves,' she added crossly. 'Is that how they teach Royal Ponies to behave at Stableside?'

Pippa could see that the argument was going nowhere and that Nightshade was getting angry.

'Stardust didn't mean to call you a thief,' Pippa said apologetically. 'We're just really worried about the horseshoes – the last one must be found before the end of the day. We didn't know anyone actually lived inside the Volcano. It's amazing here – I'd love to look around.'

Pippa smiled shyly and Nightshade smiled right back.

'Thank you. I think it's beautiful, but our home isn't to everyone's taste. I could show you around if you like?'

Pippa's face lit up.

'Yes, please!'

Eclipse stepped forward, staring at Pippa through her long, shaggy mane.

'You're from Stableside, aren't you? A right stuck-up lot, they are, down there. They think they're the only ones with a proper castle. You wait till you see what we have here. Our castle is the best! It doesn't get much grander or older. This castle was here long before Stableside. It's the very heart of Chevalia.'

'Really?' Pippa frowned. 'So why would you want to destroy the island?'

Eclipse exchanged a glance with Nightshade, who shrugged.

'What are you talking about?'

'The horseshoe that you were hiding for a game,' Pippa said carefully, 'is definitely one of eight magical horseshoes that should hang on the ancient Whispering Wall. The scientist-magician Nightingale wrote in her scrolls that Chevalia can only survive if the horseshoes' magic – and the love they capture from pony and horse lovers around the world – is renewed by the rays of the sun every Midsummer.'

Eclipse's eyes widened in alarm.

'What?' she whispered. 'Is that really true?'

Pippa nodded.

'Then the Mistress has misled us.' Nightshade looked ready to burst into tears. 'She told us that the horseshoes were symbols of power and that by hiding them, Chevalia would return to its former glory, where the Volcano was the heart of the island and every pony was equal.'

'Every pony should be equal,' Pippa agreed, 'but stealing the horseshoes isn't going to help. If you read the ancient scrolls you'll realise that before Nightingale created the horseshoes the island was just a small lump of volcanic rock – there was no former glory!'

'We must find the eighth missing horseshoe,' Stardust said urgently. 'We think it's here somewhere but we don't know where to look.'

'We'll help,' Nightshade said immediately.

Eclipse half reared up and when she spoke her voice was high with excitement.

'I think I know where it is. Nightingale had a laboratory hidden deep in the Volcano. The Mistress spends all her time there – she locked herself inside it all last night. I bet that's where she's hidden the last horseshoe. Follow me and I'll show you.'

Eclipse took off at a smart trot. In single file Nightshade, Stardust and

Misty hurried after her along several twisty, stone walkways and tunnels. The tunnels led to one side of the Volcano's inner rim and a series of caves.

'Nightingale's laboratory is in the last cave,' Eclipse said, panting slightly as she navigated the puddles of lava and the black boulders littering the ground.

Eventually they came to an archway that was fitted with a stone door and an iron latch. Eclipse expertly flipped the latch up and pushed.

The door opened with a groan. In silence everyone trooped inside and Pippa dismounted from Stardust. Long benches lined the middle of the cave and were covered with glass apparatus that was thick with dust. There were test tubes everywhere, filled with brightly coloured liquids. Pippa's throat tightened at the acid stench of chemicals. A huge cream scroll tied with a deep pink ribbon lay on top of a wooden desk. Pippa's eyes were drawn to it. Was that the original ancient scroll or just a copy? Next to it, in a frame made from volcanic rock, was a picture of a stocky-looking pony with bulging eyes.

'Divine?' Stardust asked, stepping forward.

'No, it's Nightingale,' Nightshade corrected her. 'The Mistress is a direct descendant of Nightingale. But, yes, they're very similar.'

There were further portraits of Nightingale on the walls, hanging in

ornate, gold frames. The last picture had a modern frame and was of a smaller pony with eyes that protruded even more.

'That's Divine,' Pippa exclaimed, pointing. Her voice rose suddenly. 'And hanging above the picture is the last horseshoe!'

'It is indeed.'

The voice that came from the doorway sent shivers racing along Pippa's spine. It was Baroness Divine.

'I've been expecting you.' An evil smile played on Divine's lips. Throwing back her head, she laughed triumphantly, then she shouted, 'Guards, seize them!'

Chapter 4

A group of Night Mares, wearing the guards' uniform of diamond-encrusted black sashes, charged into the laboratory and surrounded Pippa, Stardust and Misty. They marched them outside and into a long, dark tunnel lit by flickering torches. As the tunnel twisted and turned it kept splitting into more passages.

'Left, right, right, left, left, left,'

Pippa murmured to herself as she tried to memorise the route they were taking.

They were travelling downhill and, after entering a very narrow tunnel, they finally arrived at their destination.

'The dungeons,' Stardust whickered, her breath catching.

The guards roughly nudged the trio into the same cell. The door clanged shut and the key scraped in the lock.

Divine's hoof steps rang out mockingly as she started to trot away.

'You've failed.' Divine laughed.

'Wait!' cried Pippa. 'Why are you doing this to us?'

Divine swung round to face them. Drawing herself up, she said, 'Nightingale may be my distant ancestor but she was a fool. When she found magical gold in the Volcano she fashioned it into two sets of symbolic horseshoes, one set each for the King and Queen of the new island of Chevalia that the horseshoes went on to create. The island was a place where all ponies could be equal. But how could that ever be when Nightingale had decreed that there would be a King and Queen? Far better, I say, that the island remains a volcanic rock, led by only one pony. My plan is to destroy the last golden horseshoe so that Chevalia will return to what it was – a simple place with no Royal Court or Princess Ponies. There will be just one leader. Me. I shall rule the new volcanic island.'

Stardust let out a loud sob then bravely swallowed to stop any more from escaping.

'How are you going to destroy the horseshoe?' asked Pippa. Her heart hammered in her chest as she played for time.

Divine's eyes glowed in the torch-light.

'I plan to throw it into the heart of the Volcano, where the hot lava will melt it.'

'Won't that be dangerous?' Pippa asked. 'What about the magic locked inside the horseshoe?'

'Enough!' roared Divine. 'My plan is nearly complete. I don't have time to waste talking to a silly little girl.'

The Baroness clattered away, the guards following, their hooves echoing on the rough floor.

Stardust huddled in the corner of the cell and began to cry. Pippa wrapped her arms around her friend's neck. She buried her face in Stardust's silky mane, breathing in her sweet pony smell.

'Don't cry,' she said gently. 'It's not over yet.'

'But it is,' Stardust wept. 'How can we ever escape from here? Divine will destroy the eighth horseshoe and Chevalia will disappear. I'm never going to see my family again.' Her voice rose to a wail.

Pippa continued to hug her. She

wanted to say something wise and comforting but the words wouldn't come. At last she pulled away from Stardust to examine the dungeon bars. They ran from floor to ceiling and were as solid as a mountain. They didn't even rattle when Pippa tried to shake them.

'We're well and truly stuck,' she said as Misty came to stand beside her. 'Unless . . .' An idea popped into Pippa's head. With mounting excitement she said, 'Misty, could you use your unicorn magic to freeze the bars?'

Misty stared at her for a moment then a slow smile spread over her face. As Stardust realised what Pippa intended, she came to stand beside her.

'I think so,' said Misty.

As the unicorn bent her head forward, Pippa was struck by how delicate her spiralled horn looked against the thick prison bar. Could something so tiny and beautiful overcome the strength of the iron?

'Yes,' Pippa said softly.

She clenched her hands into fists. It was like good and evil. Good always won in the end if people had the courage to stand together and fight the bad.

A cracking noise reverberated around the prison cell as, slowly, the bars began to freeze. Pippa could feel the cold radiating from them.

'It's your turn now, Stardust,' said Pippa. 'Can you kick the bars out?'

Stardust shook back her long, white

mane. There was a look of determination in her brown eyes.

'Easy!' she said.

Turning her back on the bars,
Stardust lashed out with her hind hooves
and there was an ear-splitting crack.
Stardust kicked again and again.
Suddenly the bars clanged to the floor.

'Hooray!' cheered Pippa.

She scrambled up on Stardust's back.

'Now we go after Divine.'

At a fast trot Stardust and Misty fled the dungeon into the dark tunnel. Many of the flickering torches had been snuffed out. Pippa squinted as they flew along, but the passageway didn't look familiar.

'Left,' she said uncertainly, as they reached the first branch of the under-ground labyrinth.

Pippa clung on to Stardust's back, ducking her head in the places where the ceiling was low. Stardust and Misty's breathing came in noisy rasps. They continued for ages, until they

reached a crossroad of four paths.
Pippa hesitated.

'Which way?' Stardust asked, pulling
up.

Fear gripped Pippa's insides. She
didn't remember this part of the
tunnel at all. There was a buzzing noise
in her ears. Pippa shook her head
in irritation.

'Watch out!' cried a tiny voice. 'It's
meee. Your good friend Zzzimb.'

'Zimb!' Pippa's spirits soared as her
horsefly friend flew in front of her face
and landed on her nose. Pippa giggled
and crossed her eyes as she tried to
focus on him.

Zimb chuckled too then flew away
to perch on Stardust's ear.

'A little lossssssst, are we? Let Zimb help.'

There was a faint buzz and suddenly the tunnel glowed with a thousand pinpricks of light.

'Fireflies!' Pippa said, staring around in delight.

'Weee ssssaw you enter the Volcano,'

said Zimb. 'No Royal Pony has ever ventured here before. Weee guessssssed you might need help.'

'Thank you,' said Stardust.

Quickly Pippa, Stardust and Misty told Zimb why they were in the Volcano.

'Baronesssss Divine hassss assembled everyone in the castle courtyard,' said Zimb. 'Weeee sssssaw her on our way in. Hurry!'

Stardust and Misty galloped through the tunnels, led by Zimb and with the light of the fireflies showing them where to go. Together they burst into the castle courtyard. As Stardust pulled up, Pippa gasped.

'Wow!' she exclaimed, her eyes

popping at the huge crowd of Night Mares assembled in front of Divine.

No one noticed Pippa, Stardust, Misty, Zimb and the fireflies join the back of the crowd. All eyes were on Divine, who stood on a platform of black rock as she addressed the crowd. Crowning her head was the eighth golden horseshoe, glinting in the fierce light of the Volcano.

'The time has come. This Midsummer Day will go down in our history, for today marks the start of a wonderful new era for the ponies of the Volcano. We are gathered here to witness the end of the Royal Realm. Nightingale was wrong to have meddled with magic. She never should have created Chevalia and allowed ponies from the human world to come here. I will reverse her mistake. By throwing this horseshoe into the lava, our volcanic island will return to the way it was. Down with Chevalia! Long live Volcanica!'

A loud cheer resounded from the

Night Mares and they stamped their hooves with approval.

Out of the corner of her eye Pippa saw Nightshade and Eclipse huddled together. Their eyes were huge with worry and they shook their heads in disbelief.

'Only they know the truth,' Pippa said softly. 'If Divine destroys that horseshoe she'll destroy the whole island.'

Chapter 5

The cheers rose to a crescendo, and with it the courtyard darkened. Pippa stared up. What was the dark shape that was spreading closer, like spilled ink? The Night Mares fell silent. A soft whooshing noise filled the air. It reminded Pippa of wings.

'Cloud!' she exclaimed, as the silver-grey Princess Pony led a flock of flying ponies into the courtyard.

'Mum, Dad! Crystal, Cinders . . .' Stardust's voice was soft with wonder as the entire Royal Court flew into sight and hovered above them.

'I saw you enter the Volcano,' said Cloud. 'I thought you'd probably need some help.'

'And I think I saw you!' Pippa exclaimed, thinking of when they stepped into the Volcano Castle and she'd noticed something in the sky.

Cloud swooped down and rubbed her nose against first Stardust's and then Misty's nose. There was a loud crack and a bright flash of light as they both sprouted wings. Pippa adjusted her position on Stardust's back around the Princess Pony's new wings.

'You dare to invade my castle?' Divine demanded, her eyes rolling wildly. 'What's the meaning of this?'

'We've come to save Chevalia, for the good of all the ponies who live here,' Cloud replied.

'Too late!' shrieked Divine.

She tossed her head and the golden horseshoe spun into the air. It flew over the Volcano, spinning in the wind. Then it plummeted towards the fiery pit of the Volcano.

Pippa shouted to Stardust, 'After it!'

Stardust plunged down, her mane and tail flying behind her straighter than arrows. Pippa hung on tightly, gritting her teeth as the hot volcanic air washed over them. Far below she could see the molten lava glimmering red. The horse-shoe spun towards it, flashing in the fiery light.

Stardust flew even faster. Pippa could feel the pony's muscles straining as she dived towards the molten heart of the Volcano far below. Burying her left hand in Stardust's mane to anchor herself, she reached out for the spin-ning horseshoe. Her fingers brushed it but then the horseshoe spun away. Stardust flew faster still. Pippa reached out again. She was so close. Her curly hair streamed out behind her and the wind rushed in her ears. Her fingers ached as they snatched for the horse-shoe and, this time, she caught it. The horseshoe tingled in her hand as magic coursed through her fingertips. It filled her with warmth, excitement and hope.

'We did it!' she shouted.

Stardust whinnied with delight and, turning round, she soared upward. She flew over the courtyard and circled it in a lap of victory. Pippa sat tall on her back, proudly holding the horseshoe in the air for everyone to see.

'Stupid fools! You've ruined everything,' Divine shrieked with rage.

'No,' shouted Stardust. '*You* would have ruined everything, but now Chevalia is safe for us all to live in and enjoy again.'

'She's right,' Nightshade and Eclipse called out. 'The Mistress wanted the island for herself. She doesn't care what happens to us.'

The Royal Ponies flying overhead cheered wildly, but at first the Volcano ponies looked doubtfully between Divine and Stardust, unsure who to believe.

'Nightingale created the horseshoes

and Chevalia for everyone,' said Night-shade. 'Why would Divine want to destroy them unless it was for her own gain?'

It was as if the Night Mares had suddenly woken up. Their faces cleared as they understood the truth and they burst into noisy cheers.

'To Chevalia!'

The applause and cheering lasted for ages. As the noise finally died away, Stardust spoke.

'We haven't succeeded yet. For Chevalia to remain the beautiful place it is we have to hang this horseshoe on the ancient Whispering Wall by sundown.'

Queen Moonshine flew over the centre of the courtyard.

'Go quickly, my foal – time is running out. Then tonight we will celebrate, first with a Royal Concert with our new friends the unicorns, then with the Midsummer Ball. Everyone is invited – you are all my guests. From this day forth the Royal Ponies and the Volcano ponies will be better friends. The island of Chevalia belongs to us all.'

'Never!' shrieked Divine. 'I will never allow it.'

The guards surrounded Divine but she was too quick. Leaping in the air, she threw herself at Queen Moonshine. The Queen shied back in alarm, flapping her pale gold wings, but not before Divine had rubbed noses with her. There was a brilliant flash of light and a crack rent the air as the Baroness sprouted her own wings. Whinnying in triumph, Divine flew away.

'Stop her,' shouted the guards.

Ponies bolted in all directions, until the Queen called them to attention.

'Don't fear Divine. It's unlikely that she'll show her face around here again.

But if she does, we'll be ready for her. If all of us stand together we can stop her from carrying out any more evil plans.'

Pippa leaned forward and spoke into her friend's ear.

'Stardust, we have to go.'

'I know,' said Stardust. 'Hold on tight, Pippa.'

The Princess Pony's white wings flapped gracefully as she rose up and out of the Volcano and, in a straight line, headed for home.

Chapter 6

With the sun setting behind her, Stardust flew straight to Stableside Castle. Pippa urged her to fly faster as the sinking sun fell towards the horizon. As Stableside came into view, the sun was merely a golden sliver above the darkening sea. With a burst of energy, Stardust flew over the Castle walls and came to land in the Royal Courtyard. The moment her hooves touched the ground her wings disappeared. Pippa had to hold on tightly.

'There's not much time left,' Stardust said as she approached the ancient Whispering Wall.

Pippa was dimly aware of the rush of wings as the entire Royal Court returned behind them. All but Cloud landed in the courtyard – she remained above the ground, keeping her hooves tucked up beneath her.

The last rays of the sun lit the seven golden horseshoes on the wall. The magic crackled as it renewed itself but Pippa could see the bare patch of wall where the eighth horseshoe needed to be placed.

As Stardust came alongside the wall,

Pippa stood up on her back. A smile tugged at her lips as she remembered how scared she'd been the very first time she'd stood on Stardust. That had been to rescue the first golden horseshoe. She'd never completely got rid of her fear of heights but she'd come a long way to managing it. Proudly Pippa reached up and hung the golden horseshoe back where it belonged.

A sunray slanted towards it and, reaching down, kissed the horseshoe with its buttermilk glow. There was a moment of complete silence, then the Whispering Wall seemed to let out an electric sizzle. Suddenly it was as if someone had lit a thousand sparklers. The horseshoes glittered brighter than the noonday sun as their energy was fully renewed.

A huge cheer rose into the air, along with cries of 'Chevalia for ever!'

Pippa slid from Stardust's back and threw her arms around her friend's neck.

'We did it,' she sobbed. Happiness

welled inside her like a mountain stream. 'We found all the missing horseshoes. We saved Chevalia.'

Stardust nuzzled Pippa's hair.

'Thank you, Pippa,' she whickered. 'And thank you for being my best friend.'

As the very last ray of sunlight disappeared, a warm, amber light bathed the whole island. The energised horseshoes were charging the island's magic for another year. Stardust stood very still, drinking it in. All of a sudden, for Pippa, time froze. The courtyard became sketchy like a shadow, and through it she could see her family on the beach in the horseshoe-shaped cove. Her mother, brother and sister were stiller than statues, sitting with a picnic half laid out before them. A wave of longing swept over Pippa. She missed her family so much it hurt.

The light disappeared, leaving Stardust and Pippa in the darkness. Time moved on again.

'I love Chevalia,' Pippa said softly, 'but I love my own home too. It's time I returned to my family.'

'Of course,' said Stardust. 'You can't leave just yet, though.'

Pippa raised an eyebrow, making Stardust giggle.

'You can't miss the Royal Concert or the Midsummer Ball.'

There was so little time to prepare for the concert that everyone mucked in and helped. Pippa smiled as Queen Moonshine rushed past her with a huge bunch of wild flowers for King Firestar to hang around the Royal Court.

Just as the last garland was put in place the unicorns arrived from the Cloud Forest. They were greeted by courtiers who'd hurriedly changed into their best sashes and who ushered all the guests to the courtyard.

The opening bars of music soared in the air and Pippa's heart flew with it as she was carried away by the exquisite voices. Honey's coat looked pale in the moonlight as her duet approached. She needn't have worried. She sang beautifully, her confidence boosted by her unicorn twin and singing partner, Goldie. Afterwards Stardust whispered to Pippa that the concert was the best one Chevalia had ever held. Queen Moonshine thought so too.

'Much good has come from these troubled times. The ponies and unicorns who live here on Chevalia need not fear each other any more. We will work and play together for the good of the island and all ponykind.'

'What, even the Night Mares?' called a pony who hadn't flown to the Volcano with the Royal Family.

'Especially the *Volcano ponies*,' Queen Moonshine answered. 'They're no different from us.'

☆

The courtyard was full of nervous neighs but when the Volcano ponies arrived for the ball, shyly shuffling their hooves, every single pony welcomed them warmly.

Riding on Stardust's back as they danced with Prince Jet and Prince Storm, Pippa was bursting with happiness.

'Ouch!' Stardust squeaked, as Jet stepped on her hoof again.

'Sorry.' Jet blushed. 'Dancing's not really my thing.'

'Look at Crystal and Trojan.' Honey giggled, pointing to the other side of the room with a sparkly hoof.

Crystal and Trojan, the farm pony from the Grasslands, were dancing together, nuzzling as they swayed to the music.

'And there's Blossom,' Stardust said, her eyes wide with surprise. 'Who'd have thought my "clumsy" friend would be so good at dancing?!'

'It just shows you don't know what you're good at until you try different things,' Pippa said, remembering all the new things she'd tried and achieved in the last week.

There was a huge banquet at the ball. Pippa realised how hungry she was as she and Stardust ate from the flower-decorated troughs. Stardust enjoyed honey-dipped carrots and roasted oats

while Pippa polished off a glass of lemonade and a plate of fish and chips prepared especially for her.

Too soon the wonderful Midsummer evening was drawing to a close. As the ponies began to drift back to their stables, Princess Cloud swooped overhead.

'It's time, Pippa. I'm here to take you home.'

Stardust's eyes filled with tears.

'I can hardly bear to let you go,' she whinnied.

Cloud looked at her youngest sister.

'Would you like to come with us and fly your friend home?' she asked.

'Yes,' Stardust said immediately. 'I'd love that.'

Cloud flew over to rub Stardust's nose and straight away she grew a huge pair of feathery, white wings. Pippa neatly vaulted on to her back amid cries of farewell from her new friends.

Queen Moonshine's voice rose above them all.

'Goodbye, Pippa MacDonald, friend of Chevalia. You're always welcome here. Come back and see us soon.'

Pippa choked back her tears.

'I will,' she said, waving. 'Bye, Honey. Bye, Goldie. Bye, Blossom and Misty, Comet, Jet, Crystal, Storm, King Fire-star, Peggy, and goodbye, Cinders.'

With a dip of their wings, Stardust and Cloud rose into the moonlit sky and up over the glass-like sea.

'Wait,' Pippa cried, seeing two huge horse-like forms emerging from the water. 'It's Triton and Rosella!'

The giant seahorses bowed their heads as Stardust hovered above them.

'Pippa, lover of ponies, thank you for saving our island,' they called.

'Thank you for helping me,' Pippa called back.

A warm glow filled Pippa as Stardust sped away. She was glad she'd seen her seahorse friends one last time. It was with them that the entire adventure on Chevalia had started.

Stardust and Cloud flew side by side in silence. Gradually the dark night gave way to the rosy fingers of dawn and the sky lightened, until it was bright blue in the midday sun.

Cloud and Stardust both slowed, their huge wings straining with effort.

'Can you feel it?' asked Cloud. 'We've left the magic time bubble behind. You're nearly home, Pippa.'

Pippa wrapped her arms around Stardust's soft neck.

'Best friend,' she whispered, 'I'm going to miss you.'

'I'll miss you too,' Stardust said, her voice full of tears. 'But remember – it's not goodbye. We'll meet again, I know it.'

'Me too,' said Pippa.

They were hovering just above the sand by the horseshoe-shaped cove. Pippa hugged Stardust one last time and, as she did so, Stardust pressed something cold into Pippa's hand.

'To remember me by,' she said softly.

Then Pippa was sliding from Stardust's back and she dropped on to the soft sand. The whirr of wings overhead faded and, as Pippa stared into the bright blue sky, Cloud and Stardust vanished.

The beach was quiet apart from the soft hiss of the sea as it lapped against the shore. Pippa rubbed her eyes. Suddenly it was hard to imagine she'd been anywhere at all. Had she fallen asleep and had the most amazing dream? Her hand tightened around something solid. She unclenched her fingers and in her palm was Stardust's sparkly pink tiara. Pippa stared at it for a few seconds then carefully slid it into her shorts. As she did so, she realised she was back in her own clothes.

'Pippa!'

Mum was calling.

Pippa raced up the beach. Mum was just putting up a parasol over a rug that was spread with an amazing picnic. The Midsummer Ball now seemed a lifetime ago and she was ravenously hungry. Sitting down between her sister Miranda and her brother Jack, she reached for a cheese sandwich.

'This is going to be the best holiday ever,' Pippa declared.

Mum smiled as she handed round plastic beakers of squash.

'And that's even before I've told you about my final surprise.'

Pippa hurriedly swallowed a mouthful of sandwich.

'What surprise?' she asked.

'I know how much you like ponies –'

'*Love* ponies,' Pippa corrected her.

Mum smiled. 'Just down the lane from the holiday cottage there's a riding school, and guess what? I've arranged for you to have riding lessons. Wouldn't you love to learn to ride a pony?'

Pippa was speechless for a moment. Then she jumped up and hugged her mum so hard that she nearly dropped her drink.

'Thanks, Mum. It's a dream come true!'

Chevalia Now!

EXCLUSIVE
INTERVIEW WITH PIPPA
AND PRINCESS STARDUST

By Tulip Inkhoof

While Chevalia was celebrating the return of the eight magical horseshoes and enjoying the festivities, this intrepid reporter interviewed Princess Stardust and Pippa MacDonald in between the Royal Concert and the Midsummer Ball. ☆ ☆

☆ **TI (Tulip Inkhoof):** Well, you two are certainly the toast of the party. How does it feel to have saved Chevalia?

☆ **S (Princess Stardust):** It feels incredible!

☆ **P (Pippa):** It does feel great but, Stardust, let's not forget that saving the horseshoes was a team effort. We couldn't have done it by ourselves.

☆ **S:** You're right, Pippa – the entire island came together to help.

☆ **TI:** Yes, and even the Night Mares are here at the Castle for the ball?

☆ **S:** You mean the Volcano ponies, don't you? We used to call them Night Mares but that was an unfair name – we never took the time to get to know them. The Volcano ponies are the original inhabitants of Chevalia, and our very special friends.

☆ **P:** That's very grown up of you, Stardust. I think you've learnt a lot this week.

☆ **TI:** My word, have you only been on Chevalia for a week, Pippa?

☆ **P:** Yes, I can't believe it either!

☆ **S:** As soon as I saw this real, live girl on the beach that first morning, I just knew she'd come to save the island. What I didn't know was that she'd become my best friend too!

☆ **P:** I'm going to miss you so much, Stardust.

☆ **S:** Do you really have to go home to the human world? Can't you stay on Chevalia?

☆ **P:** It's so tempting, but I love my family and, even though they're not missing me because of the time bubble, the truth is that I miss them.

☆ **S:** I understand – I'd miss my family too.

4

☆ **TI:** What will you do back in the human world, Pippa? It's such a mystery to us Chevalia ponies.

☆ **P:** Well, we'll still be on holiday when I return, which I'm really looking forward to, and soon after that it's back to school.

☆ **S:** Won't you miss the excitement of Chevalia?

☆ **P:** Of course I will, but Chevalia will always be in my heart and in my memories. Besides, everything can be an adventure.

☆ **S:** That's so true – and I hope I have an adventure every single day!

☆ **TI:** Then that will give me a lot to report on!

And with that, Stardust tugged Pippa on to the dance floor for the first dance of the Midsummer Ball, leaving this young reporter to reflect on the incredibly eventful week. The week in which our beautiful island was saved, and the Royal Ponies made friends with the once mysterious, and long misunderstood, Volcano ponies.

☆ Chevalia Now, Chevalia For Ever! ☆

Queen Moonshine and **King Firestar**
invite all the ponies on Chevalia
to the **Midsummer Ball**
at Stableside Castle

A Midsummer celebration with dancing
and a delicious banquet

Please welcome the Volcano ponies
as they make their Castle debut

Dress code: wear your best sashes and sparkliest tiaras!

Dear Ponies of Chevalia

I'm writing this letter on the big wooden table in our holiday cottage and I plan to give it to Triton and Rosella to deliver before we drive back to Burlington Terrace.

It's hard to believe I've been back with my family for a whole week. In my heart it feels like I haven't left Chevalia at all.

As soon as Stardust and Cloud dropped me off at the beach, I heard Mum calling me for lunch. We had a delicious picnic on the sand with my sister Miranda and my little brother, Jack. While we were eating

I had the most wonderful surprise — Mum told me she was going to treat me to riding lessons! Every day for the past week, I had lessons with an amazing pony called Snowdrop — the pony from my dreams!

Mrs Woods, the lady who runs the riding school, encouraged us to learn eventing. Together Snowdrop and I tried dressage, cross-country and showjumping. Snowdrop and I were such a perfect match that Mrs Woods said I should return to train with Snowdrop in my next school holiday. I do hope Mum agrees! Perhaps I could visit Chevalia too? Please cross your hooves for me!

Now it's time to return to our house, to school and to normal life . . . I miss you all so much, especially Princess Stardust. To Chevalia!

Your friend
Pippa MacDonald

Princess Ponies 🐴

Look out for more fantastic adventures in Chevalia!